WELCOME TO
PASSPORT TO READING
A beginning reader's ticket to a brand-new world!

Every book in this program is designed to build read-along and read-alone skills, level by level, through engaging and enriching stories. As the reader turns each page, he or she will become more confident with new vocabulary, sight words, and comprehension.

These PASSPORT TO READING levels will help you choose the perfect book for every reader.

READING TOGETHER
Read short words in simple sentence structures together to begin a reader's journey.

READING OUT LOUD
Encourage developing readers to sound out words in more complex stories with simple vocabulary.

READING INDEPENDENTLY
Newly independent readers gain confidence reading more complex sentences with higher word counts.

READY TO READ MORE
Readers prepare for chapter books with fewer illustrations and longer paragraphs.

This book features sight words from the educator-supported Dolch Sight Words List. This encourages the reader to recognize commonly used vocabulary words, increasing reading speed and fluency.

For more information, please visit passporttoreadingbooks.com.

Enjoy the journey!

Little, Brown and Company
Hachette Book Group
1290 Avenue of the Americas, New York, NY 10104
Visit us at LBYR.com
mylittlepony.com

First Edition: October 2018

Little, Brown and Company is a division of Hachette Book Group, Inc.
The Little, Brown name and logo are trademarks of Hachette Book Group, Inc.

The publisher is not responsible for websites (or their content)
that are not owned by the publisher.

Library of Congress Control Number 2018936165

ISBNs: 978-0-316-52597-8 (pbk.), 978-0-316-45181-9 (ebook),
978-0-316-45179-6 (ebook), 978-0-316-45188-8 (ebook)

Printed in the United States of America

CW

10 9 8 7 6 5 4 3 2 1

Passport to Reading titles are leveled by independent reviewers applying the standards developed by Irene Fountas and Gay Su Pinnell in *Matching Books to Readers: Using Leveled Books in Guided Reading*, Heinemann, 1999.

Licensed By:

A Present for Everypony

adapted by **Jennifer Fox**
illustrated by **Tony Fleecs**
based on the special by **Michael Vogel**

LITTLE, BROWN AND COMPANY
New York Boston

Attention, My Little Pony fans!
Look for these words when you read this book.
Can you spot them all?

pudding

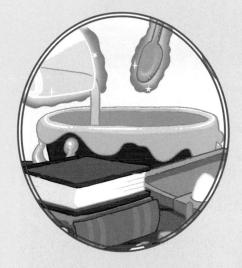

recipe

ingredients

winterchilla

"Hearth's Warming Eve is almost
here!" cries Rainbow Dash.
"There is so much to do,
and there are so many gifts to buy."

Applejack has an idea.
"Everypony, pull one name from
the hat and shop for just that pony."

"Ooh," says Pinkie Pie,
"a Hearth's Warming
Helper buddy!"
She loves Applejack's idea.

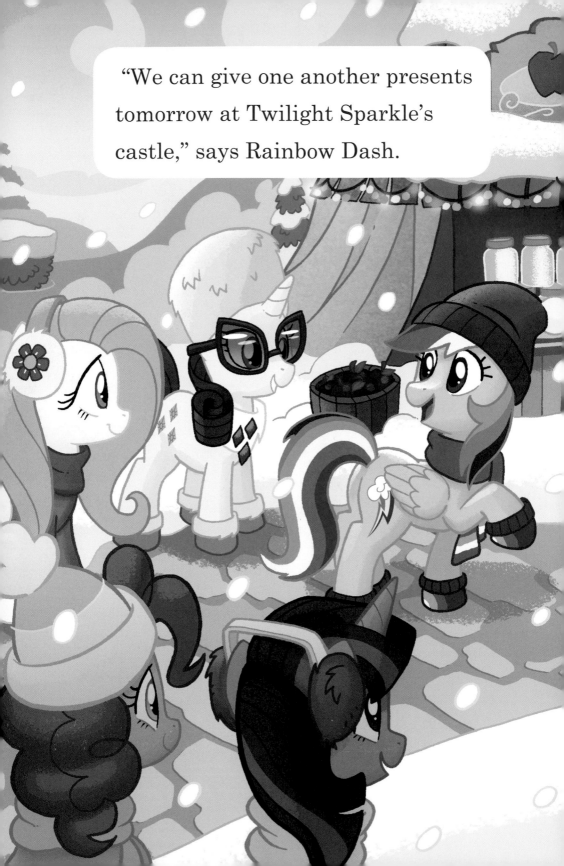

"We can give one another presents tomorrow at Twilight Sparkle's castle," says Rainbow Dash.

Everypony goes off to
find the best gift ever!

Pinkie Pie travels far away
to ask the great Gift Givers
of the Grove for help.

"Here is the perfect gift!" they say.

Pinkie peeks inside.

"I do not get it," she says.

"You will," they tell her.

Twilight searches her library.
She finds a special pudding recipe
to make for Pinkie Pie.
"It must be exactly right," she says.

Flurry Heart wants to help.

She adds in some extra ingredients!

Oh no!

Now the recipe is wrong!

Fluttershy and Applejack look
for gifts at the craft fair.

They find Flim and Flam selling
cheap dolls for too many bits.

Fluttershy and Applejack buy the dolls. They do not know what else to buy their Hearth's Warming Helper buddies.

Rainbow Dash catches a rare
winterchilla for Fluttershy.
"It is so cute!" she cries.

Not for long!
When the sun sets, the winterchilla
turns into a winterzilla!

Rarity goes to the post office to pick up the designer hat she ordered from Manehattan for Applejack.

But the package is not there!
It was sent to the wrong pony.

Hearth's Warming Eve is here! The ponies gather at Twilight's castle to give one another gifts...

...but it is a disaster!

Rarity has no hat for Applejack.

The dolls fall apart before
anypony can play with them.

Twilight's pudding for Pinkie
oozes everywhere!

The winterzilla goes wild!
"Somepony help!" Twilight cries.

Pinkie Pie grabs the box
from the great Gift Givers.

"Aha!" she yells.

"Secret ingredients!"

She tosses them in the air.

They sparkle, then settle

in the pudding.

The day is saved!
Later, the ponies sit by the fire
and eat bowls of yummy dessert.